DA NIGHT BEFORE BEFORE KRIS-MOOSE

A Christmas Poem in the Original Minnesotan

"It was so funny, it was all I could do to keep from laughing."
- Eddie Jeff Cahill

"It solved all my Christmas shopping needs."
- Deborah Johnson

"Oh jeez!"
- Sven

"What the hell??"
- Clement C. Moore
(as told to Mrs. Torvald Siggurdsson, Lutheran psychic and winner of the **1967** Lime Jello Sculpture Award for her three-dimensional Spotted Dick recipe.)

"I laughed, I cried, I felt the full range of human emotion."
- Helmar Sklarnebrutson - *Moose Monthly*

"I didn't get it, so I vetoed it."
- G.W. Bush

"It depends on your definition of 'read.' "
- B. Clinton

"An ostentatious little vintage, with hints of musk and sweat socks followed by an absolutely brutal after-taste."
- Iva Tonguesweater - *American Wine Expectorator*

DA NIGHT BEFORE KRIS-MOOSE

A Christmas Poem in the Original Minnesotan

by Terry Foy

illustrated by Delayne Hostetler

Lysander Press

Published by the Lysander Press, Ontario

First Edition
10 9 8 7 6 5 4 3 2 1

ISBN: 978-0-9737090-4-9

Printed in the United States of America.

This is a work of fiction. Names, characters, & Minnesota are products of the author's imagination, and any resemblance to actual persons, living or dead, is entirely coincidental. The Moose, however, are real.

Dedicated to Alphonse M. Goblirsch (1902-1966)

To
Sarah, Apryl and James
Every time I put pencil to paper for these illustrations
you appeared on the pages,
so I kept you there.

And thank you, Terry, for this undeserved opportunity.
Your story's funny, I drew it cute, and we're still friends.
(Right?)

D.H.

The Author would like to take this opportunity to apologize in advance to those who may justifiably take umbrage with the following palimpsest: Clement Moore, Dave Moore, Mary Tyler Moore, Dinty Moore, The Morman Tabernacle Choir, Victor Borge, Victor Hugo, Victor Victoria, Victoria, MN, Karl Rolvaag, Carl Castle, Karl Marx, Red Stanglund, Red Skelton, Red Scare, Red Wine, Red is the Color of My True Love's Eyes, Jesse Ventura, Jesse Jackson, Jesse James, Jessie's Girl, The International Brotherhood of Smelters, Sven, Ole, Lena, Udo and Toyvo and Brent who drives the monorail at the Minnesota Zoo.

No member of the "Kris-Moose" team is in any way advocating the use of snoose, snoose juice, or any combination of snoose and moose, moose and squirrel, chocolate mousse, or moose, snoose, snoose juice and loose change.

No Lutefisk was harmed in the course of this production.

'Twas da night before Kris-Moose and all tru da place

Not no von vas moovin', cause ve'd all stuffed our face.

Da stockings vas hung by da vindow vit care
'cause Papa'd vorn dem for veeks and dey needed

some air.

Da kiddies vas wrestled avay in der beds.

To get dem to stay dere, ve had to use threats.

And Mama in her face cream and me in my yammies

Had lotsa brochures for hotels in Miami.

Ven out on da lawn dere arose such a racket,

Dat I yumped outta bed and grabbed for my yacket.

I hopped to da vindow as I pulled on my pants.

My darn neighbor's dog vas in my trash cans!

My back yard vas covered vit two feet of snow
And I knew dat my lawn mower vas buried below.

I stood at da vindow and tru it took a peek;

Vat I saw dere before me left me stunned for a veek,

Vat yust so surprised me dat I svallowed my snoose

Vas a flyin' Volkswagen pulled by eight tiny moose.

Und da guy at da veel vas dressed up so slick

Dat I knew in a yiffy it must be...

Yeff Gordon, no...

Saint Nick!

Like smelt in da springtime dose mooses dey came,
Und he vistled and shouted and called dem by name:

"Now Udo, now Toyvo, now Sven and now Ole,

On Yasha, on Heifitz, on Spot and Guacamole!

To da top a da house, to da top a da trees!

If ya don't vant to crash, you better kick up dose knees!"

Like a flock of crazed geese dat don't know vat to do,
Dey circled da house like some drunk on a Ski-Doo.

Und den vat I heard t'veen da laughing and yinkles,

Vas tirty-two moose feet scrapin' my shinkles.

Vell, I scratched on my head and felt like a chump -

Down da chimney St. Nicholas fell vid a *tump*.

He vas dressed all in flannel, dat vas his attire,
And he smoldered a bit cause he sat in da fire.

A whole bunch a toys he had in a sack,
And he looked like a burglar ven he opened his pack.

But he a had nice face, though his manner vas brisk.

And his tummy it yiggled like fresh lutefisk.

A big hunk a snoose he had vedged in von cheek,

And it vas so big he vas unable to speak,

So he drooled yust a bit, vent straight to his vork,
Filled all dem stockings and turned like a yerk,

And putting a hanky in front of his nose
and giving a *honk!*

Up da chimney he rose!

He yumped in his Bug,

to his team gave a yell,

And avay dey all flew like a bat outta...

Fargo!

He spat out da vindow,

says, "Nice to have metcha!

Have a svell Kris-Moose,

YA SURE, YOU BETCHA!"

The End.

About the
Author

Terry Foy grew up in Minneapolis, Minnesota, went to college, and, in spite of the best efforts of the faculty, received a B.A. in theater from St. Cloud State University. He is a prime example of the damage a liberal arts education can do. He has been performing as Zilch the Tory Steller at Renaissance Festivals for the last three decades, including festivals in Arizona, Colorado, Florida, Georgia, Massachusetts, Minnesota, North Carolina, North and South Dakota, and Texas. He has performed at the "Robin Hood Festival" in Sherwood Forest, Nottinghamshire, England. His renditions of Rindercella, Loldigocks and the Bee Threars, and Jomeo and Ruliet have tickled audiences at Theaters, Civic Celebrations, Corporate Parties and Shopping Malls from coast to coast. He has never held a real job. He currently resides in Mankato, Minnesota.

About the Illustrator

Delayne Hostetler was once a little girl nicknamed 'Punky' who sat for hours in front of a black-and-white TV watching such local Minnesota favorites as *Axel and His Dog, Grandpa Ken,* and *Lunch With Casey* while drawing horses in her sketchbook. A childhood highlight was being a guest on the *Dave Lee & Pete Show* and having her pigtail tugged by Pete the Penguin! She has since grown up, is still an artist, and has even been known to occasionally eat lutefisk at Christmas. Delayne lives in Anoka, Minnesota with her artist partner James Henke who is a lifelong Minnesotan too, doesn't eat lutefisk at Christmastime or otherwise, and was once a guest on *Romper Room* during which he 'drove' the milk truck. (This, according to him, trumps any *Dave Lee & Pete* nonsense.) More examples of Delayne's artwork can be seen at her website: www.mayfaireart.com.

Printed in the United States
130158LV00001B/221-320/A

9 780973 709049